# JUST
# JOSEFINA

JOSEFINA · 1824

BY VALERIE TRIPP

ILLUSTRATIONS JEAN-PAUL TIBBLES

VIGNETTES PHILIP HOOD, SUSAN McALILEY

THE AMERICAN GIRLS COLLECTION®

Visit our Web site at **americangirl.com**

Printed in Singapore.
02 03 04 05 06 07 08 09 TWP 10 9 8 7 6 5 4 3 2 1

The American Girls Collection® and logo, American Girls Short Stories,™
the American Girl logo, Josefina,® and Josefina Montoya®
are trademarks of Pleasant Company.

**Library of Congress Cataloging-in-Publication Data**

Tripp, Valerie, 1951–
Just Josefina / by Valerie Tripp ;
illustrations by Jean-Paul Tibbles ; vignettes, Philip Hood, Susan McAliley.
p. cm. — (The American girls collection)
Summary: In 1824 New Mexico, nine-year-old Josefina is happy when
her grandparents and aunt come to visit, but she thinks she must choose
between meeting her grandmother's expectations and being true to herself.
Includes historical notes on women's rights in New Mexico in 1824
as well as a recipe for empanaditas.

ISBN 1-58485-478-2
[1. Self-acceptance—Fiction. 2. Grandmothers—Fiction.
3. Mexican Americans—Fiction. 4. Ranch life—New Mexico—Fiction.
5. New Mexico—History—To 1848—Fiction.]
I. Tibbles, Jean-Paul, ill. II. Hood, Philip, ill. III. McAliley, Susan, ill.
IV. Title. V. Series.
PZ7+ [Fic]—dc21 2001036653

# The
# AMERICAN GIRLS
# COLLECTION™

OTHER AMERICAN GIRLS
SHORT STORIES:

PICTURE CREDITS

The following individuals and organizations have generously given permission to reprint illustrations contained in "Looking Back": p. 38—Museum of New Mexico, Neg. 31501; Landscape, © Liz Hymans/CORBIS; p. 40—Center for Southwest Studies, The University of New Mexico, Neg. 000-179-0635; p. 41—New Mexico State Records Center & Archives, SANMI #351; p. 46—Detail from painting by Carlos Nebel, ca. 1830; p. 47—© Bob Rowan: Progressive Image/CORBIS; p. 48—Photography by Jamie Young.

# TABLE OF CONTENTS

### PAPÁ
*Josefina's father, who
guides his family
and his rancho with
quiet strength.*

### ANA
*Josefina's oldest sister,
who is married and has
two little boys.*

### JOSEFINA
*A nine-year-old girl
whose heart and
hopes are as big as
the New Mexico sky.*

### FRANCISCA
*Josefina's fifteen-year-old
sister, who is headstrong
and impatient.*

### CLARA
*Josefina's practical,
sensible sister, who is
twelve years old.*

**TÍA DOLORES**
*Josefina's aunt, who
has lived far away in
Mexico City for ten years.*

**ABUELITO**
*Josefina's grandfather,
a trader who lives in
Santa Fe.*

**ABUELITA**
*Josefina's gracious,
dignified grandmother,
who values tradition.*

Josefina and her family speak Spanish, so you'll see some Spanish words in this book. If you can't tell what a word means from reading the story or looking at the illustrations, you can turn to the "Glossary of Spanish Words" on page 56. It will tell you what the word means and how to pronounce it.

Remember that in Spanish, "j" is pronounced like "h." That means Josefina's name is pronounced "ho-seh-FEE-nah."

# JUST
# JOSEFINA

Josefina stood outside the gate to the house and leaned forward, shading her eyes. Did she see a cloud of dust on the horizon? She held her breath and listened. Surely that low rumble she heard was the sound of a wagon lumbering toward the *rancho*. Oh, she hoped so! All day while doing her chores, Josefina had been on the lookout, watching and listening for a wagon. Josefina bounced on her toes, too excited to stand still. It was always a treat when her grandparents, Abuelito and Abuelita, came from their home in Santa Fe to visit. And today, *today*, they were bringing Tía Dolores with them. Josefina couldn't wait.

Josefina felt gentle hands on her shoulders. She turned and saw her papá. Papá didn't say anything, but he stood behind Josefina and watched the dust cloud come closer and closer until, at last, the noisy wagon appeared in the middle of it. They saw Abuelito take off his hat and wave it at them.

Josefina bounced again. By now her sisters, Ana, Francisca, and Clara, were lined up next to Papá to greet their guests. Josefina knew her sisters wanted

to dash down the road as much as she
did, waving their arms and shouting
their happy hellos. But they all knew that
would not be proper. So they stood, polite
and impatient, while the wagon lurched
and rattled to the gate and stopped.

"Welcome," said Papá. He held his
hand up to help Tía Dolores down from
the wagon.

"*Gracias*," said Tía Dolores. She
smiled, and all the sisters beamed. They
were so glad to see her! "And thank you
for your kind welcome," she added.

"*Sí, sí*, we thank you," said Abuelito
as he climbed down from the wagon.
"And we thank God for our safe journey."

"Safe it may have been," said

Abuelita, thumping her skirts so that her own private cloud of dust rose up around her. "Comfortable it was not."

"Ah, my dear!" exclaimed Abuelito. "But here we are! And what an important day this is. For the first time, the first time *ever*, our whole family here on earth is gathered in one spot. How blessed we are! How—"

"Yes, dear," Abuelita spoke over him. "Very true. But now I must get inside."

Josefina stepped forward. "May I help you, Abuelita?" she asked.

"Ah, yes. Gracias, dear child," said Abuelita. "I'm so coated with dust, I feel like a floury *tortilla*." As Josefina helped her grandmother out of the wagon,

*"Gracias, dear child," said Abuelita.*
*"I'm so coated with dust, I feel like a floury tortilla."*

Abuelita spoke over her shoulder to
 Abuelito. "Bring my traveling bag," she ordered him.
The sisters exchanged
little half-smiles. They were quite used to
the way Abuelita bossed everyone, even
Abuelito. When she was safely on the
ground, Abuelita let go of Josefina and
picked up her skirts in both hands. Like
a stately queen, she sailed through the
gate with Abuelito following after. But
Josefina and her sisters stayed behind
with Tía Dolores and Papá, who was
directing the servants to unload Tía
Dolores's huge trunk from the wagon
and carry it to the room that
was to be hers.

*That trunk has traveled a long, long way,*
Josefina thought. *I wonder what's inside it.*

For ten years, since before Josefina
was born, Tía Dolores had lived in Mexico
City. Then, at the end of the summer, she
had surprised everyone by returning to
New Mexico with Abuelito's caravan.
Now it was early fall, and after a short
visit to Santa Fe, Tía Dolores had come
to live on Papá's rancho with Josefina
and her sisters. Their mother had died
more than a year ago, and the sisters
were struggling to manage the household. Tía Dolores had promised to stay
as long as they needed her.

Josefina was even more curious
about her tall, energetic aunt than she

was about the trunk. Tía Dolores was not beautiful, exactly. But there was a liveliness about her and a look of alert intelligence that Josefina liked. Tía Dolores did not act like other women Josefina knew. She walked across the courtyard with long, confident strides and asked Papá questions about the rancho in a very direct and interested way.

After her trunk was put in its place and Papá and the servants had left the room, Tía Dolores turned to the girls. "I've got so many things to show you," she said. "Do you want to help me unpack?"

"Sí," all four sisters said eagerly.

Tía Dolores unfastened the straps and lifted the lid of her trunk.

"Ohhh," sighed Ana, Francisca, Clara, and Josefina in one voice. It was as if Tía Dolores had opened a treasure chest. The sisters breathed in a luxurious scent as luscious as roses in sunshine. The trunk seemed to overflow with colors. Francisca, always the boldest, stepped closer.

"Go ahead," Tía Dolores encouraged her, smiling.

Francisca took a beautiful red shawl out of the trunk. She wrapped it around her shoulders, then twirled so that the fringe on the shawl fluttered. Tía Dolores and all the sisters laughed aloud in delight. After that, Ana shyly tried a hair

9

comb, and Clara inspected a lovely little
case that held shiny scissors and pins.
Josefina saw a sash made of material as
orange as the setting sun. She lifted it out
of the trunk and was surprised to feel
how light it was. The material was satiny
to the touch and smooth as water.

"Look at this, Josefina," Tía Dolores

said. She handed Josefina a small book bound in soft leather. Josefina had seen very, very few books in her life and never one bound so prettily as this. "Open it," said Tía Dolores.

Josefina started to. But just then, Papá stuck his head in the door.

"Josefina," he said. "Abuelita is waiting."

"Oh!" exclaimed Josefina. "Sí, Papá." Quickly, she handed the orange sash and the pretty book to Tía Dolores. "I must go, Tía Dolores," she said.

"Certainly," said Tía Dolores.

Josefina hurried as she crossed the courtyard to Abuelita's room. She'd been so distracted by Tía Dolores and her fascinating trunk that she had forgotten her special duty. She was *always* the one who helped Abuelita get settled when she came to visit.

"Ah, here you are!" said Abuelita when Josefina came in. "You're the only one who can soothe my jangled nerves after that long, hot journey. Just you, Josefina. You're patient and quiet, like your dear mamá."

Josefina felt a rush of love for Abuelita. What an honor it was to be singled out from among her sisters to be Abuelita's preferred helper! And how kind Abuelita was to say that Josefina was like Mamá. No praise could please Josefina more. No praise could make her prouder.

Quietly, Josefina poured Abuelita a
drink of cold, refreshing lemon water.
Then she brought Abuelita a bowl
of cool water that had mint
leaves floating in it. She
gave Abuelita a clean linen
hand cloth and a bar of lavender soap.
While Abuelita washed off the dust of
the road, Josefina unpacked her traveling
bag for her. Carefully, Josefina shook the
wrinkles out of Abuelita's dark, somber
clothes and hung them on pegs. Neatly,
she folded Abuelita's black *rebozo* and
placed it on the *banco*.

"Thank you, dear child," said
Abuelita. "I'll rest now." She sank back
into her chair, put her feet up on a stool,

13

and closed her eyes.

Josefina knelt on the floor next to Abuelita's chair. As she had done so many times before, she sang softly to ease Abuelita to sleep. She sang the same slow, soft, sweet song she always sang for Abuelita. But suddenly, her song was interrupted. Happy whoops of laughter looped across the courtyard. Josefina stopped singing and listened to her sisters and Tía Dolores laughing together. *What are they all having so much fun about?* she wondered.

Abuelita patted Josefina's hand. "Ignore those noisy hens!" she said.

Josefina tried, but she couldn't ignore the laughter. She couldn't ignore an itchy impatience she felt, either. *I wish Abuelita would hurry up and fall asleep so that I could go join my sisters and Tía Dolores,* Josefina thought. *I wish . . .* She stopped herself. She was shocked at her own thoughts and shivered as if to shake off a terrible suspicion. Maybe she wasn't the patient and quiet child Abuelita thought she was. Maybe she wasn't like Mamá after all.

A few days later, Josefina and her sisters spent a happy afternoon picking apples with Tía Dolores. Neighbors were coming that evening, and the cook needed apples to make *empanaditas* to serve.

"I'm looking forward to seeing everyone tonight," said Tía Dolores as they walked back to the rancho from the orchard with their baskets full.

It was the custom at harvest time for neighbors to help one another. Tonight everyone was gathering at Papá's to help string chile peppers into *ristras*. People told jokes and stories as they worked, and sometimes there was music.

"I hope there'll be dancing," said Francisca. "I'd love to show off that new dance you taught us, Tía Dolores." She held her basket of apples steady on her head with one hand, held her skirt with her other hand, and danced along the road humming the music. It looked like so much fun that soon Ana, Clara, and Josefina were dancing, too. Josefina skipped and twirled and danced ahead of the others, her feet flying all the rest of the way to the gate of the house.

"That was wonderful, Josefina!" said Tía Dolores.

"You do that dance almost as well as I do," said Francisca, who prided herself on being the best dancer in the family. "And you surely do it *faster* than all of the rest of us." Clara and Ana agreed.

Josefina twirled once more, then curtsied. "Gracias," she said. She liked the dance. It was exuberant and a little wild. It made her feel happy and free.

Inside the gate, Abuelita met them. "Look at you!" she said, smiling but sounding a little exasperated. "Your clothes are mussed. Your hands are scratched. You have twigs in your hair."

"We've been picking apples," said Tía Dolores.

"And now your noses are as red as apples," said Abuelita, shaking her head. "I gave up on your ruddy complexion long ago, Dolores. But, girls, how many times have I told you to shade your faces? You'll ruin your skin." Abuelita sighed. "Hurry along now, and tidy yourselves," she ordered, fluttering her hands at the sisters as if she were scattering chickens.

"Our guests will be here soon. Josefina, you come with me."

Obediently, Josefina followed Abuelita into her cool, shadowy room.

"I have something special for you to wear tonight," said Abuelita. She handed Josefina a pretty skirt. It was blue with a shiny black ribbon at the hem and black flowers scattered all over it like flowers in a field.

"Oh, Abuelita!" said Josefina, delighted. "It's beautiful. Gracias."

"Put it on," said Abuelita.

Josefina slipped off the old skirt she'd worn apple picking and carefully stepped into the new one. She had to

19

hold her breath to button the skirt. It fit, but only just. It was very, very tight around her waist.

But Abuelita did not notice. "That skirt belonged to your mamá," she said, her eyes bright. "I want you to have it because you remind me of her so much. You have the same small hands and round cheeks, the same sweet voice, and the same sweet disposition. She was shy and obedient like you." Abuelita smiled. "Not like my adventurous Dolores!"

"Gracias, Abuelita," said Josefina again, straight from her heart. She was grateful for Abuelita's gift and even more thankful for Abuelita's compliments. She hugged her grandmother—but carefully.

She did not want to pop the button off her beautiful blue skirt.

"Are you feeling all right, Josefina?" Tía Dolores asked her that evening. "You are so quiet. And you haven't eaten a bite."

Josefina blushed. "I am very well, thank you, Tía Dolores," she said, even though the truth was that she could hardly breathe. She could not tell Tía Dolores that she wasn't talking or eating because Mamá's skirt was strangling her around the waist! She could not bend or stoop. She had to sit uncomfortably stiff and straight, which made it hard to

string the chiles. She had to say no thank
you when some of the children invited
her to play a running game. And when
the grownups began telling jokes and
stories, Josefina couldn't let herself laugh
too much or it would strain her skirt.

It was hard not to laugh, especially
when Abuelito told everyone's favorite
story, the one about the time he brought
Tía Dolores's piano from Mexico City.
Of course, Josefina and everyone else

had heard many times how
thieves attacked the caravan but were frightened
away by the thunderous
sound of the piano falling off a wagon.
But Abuelito made the story funnier

every time he told it. Besides, everyone was very interested in Tía Dolores's piano. Most of the guests had never seen or heard a piano in their lives.

"Will you play your piano for us?" Papá asked Tía Dolores after Abuelito had finished his story.

"I'd be pleased to," Tía Dolores said. She rose and led the way to the *gran sala*.

At first, everyone stood politely and listened to the music. But then Tía Dolores began to play a dance tune that was so lively, no one could resist it. Couples began dancing. Those too old to dance sat and clapped and nodded their heads in time to the music. Those too young to dance, like Clara and Josefina,

tapped their feet and jigged in place.
Soon, the whole room was full of move-
ment. The music swooped and swirled
around them, encircling them with its
energy. One dance led to another, and
another.

Josefina moved next to the piano so
that she could watch Tía Dolores's fingers
fly over the keys. Suddenly, Tía Dolores
began to play the music that went with
the new dance she'd taught Josefina and
her sisters.

"Josefina," said Tía Dolores over the
music. "Show everyone the new dance
I taught you. You dance it so well."

Before Josefina could answer,
Abuelita spoke up from her seat near

the piano. "Gracious, Dolores!" Abuelita exclaimed. "You've brought new notions from Mexico City as well as new dances. It is not proper for Josefina to dance in front of company. She is too young."

"But, Mamá," said Tía Dolores, "the guests are all old friends and neighbors."

"Nevertheless!" said Abuelita sternly. "Josefina is not allowed to dance. She obeys the rules even if you don't. In any case, little Josefina is far too shy." Abuelita turned to Josefina and said in a voice that sounded confident of being obeyed, "You wouldn't dream of dancing, would you, pet?"

But dreaming seemed to be just what Josefina was doing. Because much to her own surprise, she found herself stepping out onto the floor. As if the music had enchanted her, she began to dance. Josefina's feet hardly touched the ground, she skipped and spun and danced so fast. How wonderful it felt! Josefina listened to the wild, exuberant music and let it carry her without think- ing. People clapped for her and stamped their feet so that the floor shook. Soon they joined the dance, too, and Josefina was surrounded by swirling skirts and dancing feet.

Faster and faster Josefina danced until—*pop!* The button on Mamá's skirt shot off. No one else noticed, but Josefina stopped dancing. She clutched her skirt

*Josefina's feet hardly touched the ground, she skipped
and spun and danced so fast. How wonderful it felt!*

to her waist and watched the button spin across the floor and skitter like a bug past the dancers' shoes until it stopped dead, right at Abuelita's feet. With a cold and disapproving frown, Abuelita picked up the button and put it in her pocket.

Josefina's heart thudded as she realized what she had done. She had disobeyed and disappointed Abuelita. Now Abuelita would never feel the same way about her again.

When the dance ended, the evening did, too. Reminding one another that tomorrow was a working day, the guests said good-bye and thank you to Papá, Abuelita, Abuelito, and Tía Dolores. They strolled home under the starry sky, still humming or whistling the music that Tía Dolores had played. When the last guest was gone and the last note had faded away, Josefina followed Abuelita to her room to sing her to sleep as she always did.

But Abuelita dismissed her. "I don't need you tonight, Josefina," she said coolly. She closed her door, leaving Josefina alone.

Josefina crossed the courtyard to the room she shared with her sisters. Sadly, she took off the beautiful blue skirt, folded it carefully, and put it away.

Josefina went to bed, but her heart was so heavy that she couldn't sleep. All night she lay awake thinking. By morning she had decided what she must do. At dawn, she rose quietly and dressed in her work clothes. She picked up the blue skirt and held it close to her chest. Silently, she tiptoed across the courtyard to Abuelita's room. She gave the skirt one last hug, then slowly bent down to put it outside Abuelita's door.

Suddenly, the door opened.

Josefina looked up. Abuelita was standing in the doorway of her room. She seemed small and shadowy in the early morning light.

"I have been waiting for you, Josefina," said Abuelita. "Come in."

Abuelita lit a candle. Then she sat tiredly in her chair and motioned for

Josefina to sit on the floor beside her.
Josefina knew she must not speak first.
She waited anxiously for what Abuelita
was going to say.

"Dear child," Abuelita began. Then
she stopped.

Josefina burst out, "Oh, Abuelita.
I'm sorry. I know I disappointed you

when I danced. But Tía Dolores's music made me feel so wonderful, I *had* to dance. I know Mamá never would have done such a thing." Josefina sighed. "I've always been so honored when you've said that I'm like Mamá. But I've learned something about myself. In some ways I am like Mamá, but in some ways I am not." Josefina put the blue skirt on Abuelita's lap. "This is a beautiful skirt, Abuelita," she said. "But it doesn't really fit me. Do you want it back?"

Abuelita stroked the skirt. "I've learned something, too," she said. "I miss your Mamá so much that I look every-where for reminders of her." Abuelita smiled at Josefina, but it was a sad smile.

"I saw many reminders in you, and they comforted me. But that wasn't fair of me. You're not like anyone else, nor should you be. You're yourself, and that's perfect. I love you because you are you."

Josefina rose up on her knees and hugged Abuelita around the waist.

"And as for your blue skirt," said Abuelita, sounding more like her usual bossy self, "you must sew this back on immediately." She pulled the button out of her pocket. "But put it in a different place so that the waistband is looser." She raised her eyebrows as she said, "And you had better sew it on good and tight, in case you decide to dance again."

"Sí," said Josefina happily.

Abuelita was happy, too. "The skirt belongs to you now," she said. "You must fix it so that it fits you and no one else—just you, just Josefina."

# VALERIE TRIPP

At 9    Now

My daughter, Katherine, says she has hair like mine and eyes like my husband's. But I tell her that everything about her is all hers. Like Josefina, she is perfect because she's herself—just Katherine.

*Valerie Tripp has written forty-four books in The American Girls Collection, including ten about Josefina.*

Looking
Back
1824

# A PEEK INTO
## THE PAST

Women's
Rights in
1824

Josefina comes from a long line of
strong, spirited women. Like Abuelita,
Tía Dolores, and Ana, New Mexican
women in the early 1800s had many
responsibilities. They ran large
households and worked with
their husbands on ranchos,
while also raising and educating
their children. These women

found strength in their faith and family relationships, just as American women of the time did. But New Mexican women had rights and freedoms that American women would not have for many years.

When an American woman in 1824 got married, she took her husband's last name and lost any legal rights of her own. A married woman could not buy or sell property, and her husband took control of any property that was hers before the marriage. She

*Land was the most common property that women—both American and New Mexican— brought into a marriage.*

could not sign legal documents or appear in courts of law. And although she might work outside the home, any wages she earned were controlled by her husband.

New Mexican women, in contrast, had rights that were deeply rooted in Spanish tradition. They kept their maiden names after marriage. They also kept any property that was theirs before marriage,

*A New Mexican wedding in the late 1800s*

such as money or jewelry passed down to them by their mothers. Whatever a woman owned, she could make decisions about without consulting her husband. She could sell property or pass it down to her own daughter by drawing up a *will*, a document that says what should happen to a person's possessions when she dies.

Under Mexican law, women could have wills created in their own names. The property described in the will could

*Wills included long lists of possessions.*

be anything from land and herds of animals to the clothes and household goods the woman owned at the time of her death. One will written in 1830 included a silk jacket, a fringed shawl, and "three petticoats of coarse cotton—used."

Mexican law also gave women the right to protect their possessions. They could *sue,* or take to court, anyone who threatened their property. Some women sued their own husbands! Doña Gregoria Quintana took her husband to court when he sold her grain mill without her consent. The court ordered that

*Many women owned silk shawls called* **mantóns** *(mahn-TOHNS).*

the new owner of the mill grind a portion of grain for Doña Gregoria each year until her death. Another woman took her husband to court for gambling away her burro. The court ordered that the burro be returned to the wife and fined the husband two pesos for gambling.

New Mexican women in 1824 were free to work outside the home and to keep their earnings. Some, like Doña Gregoria, even owned their own businesses. One of the most successful of

*A sturdy burro was valuable property.*

these women was Gertrudis Barceló, known as Doña Tules (TOO-lehs). She owned a gambling house in Santa Fe—an unusual business for women of the time. Doña Tules was a skilled card dealer and a smart businesswoman. Her gambling house was popular among Mexican and American soldiers, and Doña Tules became a trusted advisor to both. She also became quite wealthy. When the U.S. Army needed money, it turned to Doña Tules for help!

Many people respected Doña Tules's independence and spirit, but American traders were shocked to see women in gambling halls, smoking and playing cards with men. Americans were also surprised by the clothing worn by New Mexican

*Doña Tules, the woman who dared to do men's work*

women: loose cotton blouses and skirts that revealed their ankles. This clothing was practical in the warm Southwest, but it was very different from the corsets and hoopskirts worn by American women at the time.

As traders brought American goods and ideas south, the free-flowing clothing of New Mexican women gave way to more confining American styles. When New Mexican women became American citizens in 1848, they lost other freedoms, too. Their legal rights didn't hold up in American courts, and women lost some of their independence. But they never lost their spirit. The courage and determination shown by these early New Mexican women are still alive in Hispanic women of today.

*This young doctor follows in the footsteps of her Hispanic ancestors, many of whom worked as midwives and healers.*

An
American
Girls
Pastime

# MAKE APPLE EMPANADITAS

*Dried apples make these plump
tarts supersweet!*

During the fall harvest, Josefina and
her family picked apples from the orchard
to make little fruit pies, called *empanaditas*.
They also preserved some of the apples
by slicing and stringing them up to dry.
During the cold months, the Montoyas
could eat the apple slices as a sweet treat
or could boil them in water to use in
empanaditas. Make these little tarts using
dried apples, just as Josefina might have!

# You Will Need:

 *An adult to help you*

**Ingredients**

4 refrigerated
piecrusts

4 ounces dried apples

1 cup sugar

½ teaspoon ground
cinnamon

¼ teaspoon
ground cloves

1 egg

1 tablespoon water

Flour for rolling
out dough

**Equipment**

Saucepan

Wooden spoon

Colander

Paring knife

Cutting board

Blender or food processor

Measuring cups
and spoons

Medium mixing bowl

Small bowl

Wire whisk

Rolling pin

3-inch round cookie cutter

Pastry brush

Fork

Cookie sheet

Potholders

1. Place the dried apples in the saucepan and cover them with water. Have an adult help you bring the water to a boil. Simmer the apples for 30 minutes or until tender, stirring occasionally.

2. Have an adult drain the water from the apples. Allow them to cool. Have an adult cut the apples into small pieces and puree them in a blender or food processor until only small lumps remain.

**3.** Stir together the apples, ½ cup of sugar, and the cinnamon and cloves in the medium bowl. Set aside the remaining ½ cup of sugar.

**4.** Preheat the oven to 375 degrees. Spread the piecrust flat on a floured surface. If the crust has crimped edges, roll the edges flat with the rolling pin.

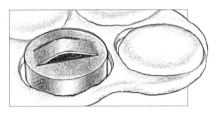

**5.** Use the cookie cutter to cut as many circles as you can out of the crust.

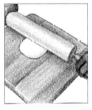

**6.** Roll the dough scraps into a ball. Flatten it slightly with your hand, then roll it from the center to the edges with the rolling pin until the dough is about ¼ inch thick. Repeat steps 5 and 6 until all the dough is used.

**7.** To make an egg wash to seal the pastry, crack the egg into a small bowl. Beat the egg with the wire whisk, and stir in the water. Use the pastry brush to paint egg wash around the edge of each circle.

**8.** Put 1 rounded teaspoon of apple filling in the center of each circle. Fold the circle in half, and press the edges together with your fingers.

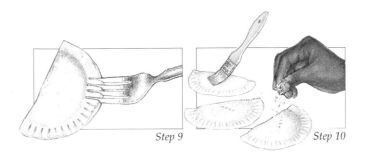

Step 9

Step 10

9. Dip the tip of the fork in flour, and press the fork down around the edges of each empanadita. Prick the center of each pastry with the fork.

10. Brush egg wash over the top of the empanaditas, and sprinkle them with sugar. Place them on an ungreased cookie sheet, and bake for 15 to 20 minutes or until lightly browned. Have an adult remove the empanaditas from the oven. Let them cool before serving.

# GLOSSARY OF SPANISH WORDS

**banco** *(BAHN-koh)*—a low bench built into the wall

**empanadita** *(em-pah-nah-DEE-tah)*—a small pie or tart filled with fruit, nuts, or meat

**gracias** *(GRAH-see-ahs)*—thank you

**gran sala** *(grahn SAH-lah)*—the biggest room in the house, used for special events and formal occasions

**mantón** *(mahn-TOHN)*—an embroidered silk shawl

**rancho** *(RAHN-cho)*—a farm or ranch where crops are grown and animals are raised

**rebozo** *(reh-BO-so)*—a long shawl worn by girls and women

**ristra** *(REE-strah)*—a string of chiles

**sí** *(SEE)*—yes

**tortilla** *(tor-TEE-yah)*—a kind of flat, round bread made of corn or wheat